Dear Reader,

Everyone has a special talent. Sometimes it takes our family and friends to help us understand what our talent is. When I was younger I had always wanted to play the guitar, but when it came time to choose an instrument to learn, I chose the trombone. I picked it because it was the biggest instrument in our school band and looked like it would be a lot of fun to play. I took lessons and played the trombone all through high school. I even played in my school's marching band.

I have a great appreciation for musical talent, which is why I thought it would be fun for Rhino to learn how to play the guitar for his school talent show, even though he was already taking trombone lessons. To this day, I enjoy listening to music while I'm on my way to baseball practice or a baseball game. When I hear certain songs on the radio, it brings me back to the days I played the trombone, marched in the marching band, and took music lessons in between schoolwork and baseball practice. It's not always easy, but whatever your talent may be, practice it to succeed, and don't forget to always have fun.

LITTLE

Rhino

by RYAN HOWARD
and KRYSTLE HOWARD

● BOOK FOUR ●
THE TALENT SHOW

SCHOLASTIC INC.

To those who build the confidence to believe in themselves.

—R.H. & K.H.

Text copyright © 2016 by Ryan Howard
Illustrations © 2016 by Scholastic Inc.

This book is being published simultaneously in hardcover by Scholastic Press.

ISBN 978-1-338-05223-7

10 9 8 7 6 5 4 3 2 1   16 17 18 19 20

Printed in the U.S.A.   40
First printing 2016

Book design by Christopher Stengel

· CHAPTER 1 ·
Hidden Talents

Little Rhino watched the baseball sail high over the field. He'd hit it hard, but it was drifting toward the foul pole.

Stay fair, he thought. He felt a surge of energy as the ball flew past the pole, clearing the right-field fence in fair territory.

Home run!

Rhino smiled. This was batting practice, so he didn't run around the bases. But the excitement was there anyway.

"One more swing," said Coach Ray, who was pitching.

Rhino drew back his bat and waited. He'd hit three balls over the fence while at bat. Rhino had turned into a strong hitter during his first baseball season, and his confidence grew with every swing.

Just like a major leaguer, he thought.

The next pitch was straight down the middle and waist high. Rhino clobbered it, sending it streaking toward center field. It bounced near the top of the fence and rebounded onto the grass. Another solid hit.

Rhino walked to the dugout and went to bump fists with his best friend, Cooper. But instead Cooper raised a finger to his lips, signaling to Rhino to stay quiet. Cooper jutted his chin toward the only other player in the dugout.

Carlos sat alone on the bench, singing softly. His blue Mustangs cap was pulled low over his forehead.

Rhino raised his eyebrows. Carlos was one of the smallest players on the team, and he was one of the quietest kids Rhino knew. But his singing voice was surprisingly good. Clear and tuneful.

Carlos was singing a hymn. But then he switched to another song, more upbeat and soulful.

Rhino laughed.

Carlos stopped singing and clamped his mouth shut.

"Don't stop," Rhino said. "You have a great voice. I was only laughing because I was surprised to hear it."

Carlos looked down, but he smiled. "Forgot where I was for a minute," he said.

"Sounded like you could have been on a stage!" Cooper said. "Are you a singer?"

"Sort of," Carlos replied. "I've been in our church choir since kindergarten. But I've never sung a solo or anything like that."

"You should be performing," Rhino said. "The school talent show is coming up. You'd win with a voice like that!"

Carlos laughed and shook his head. "I'd have stage fright in a talent show. Wouldn't be able to make a peep."

"You need a backup band to give you confidence," Cooper said. "I play drums. Do you play an instrument?"

Clang! A baseball rattled off the dugout fence, making them jump. Their teammate Dylan was at bat, and he'd lined a hard foul ball in their direction.

"Wake up in there!" Dylan called.

"Try hitting it straight!" Rhino yelled back.

Dylan grinned. "Just wanted to make sure you were paying attention," he said.

They watched as Dylan smacked the next pitch toward the shortstop. Then Rhino and Cooper turned back to Carlos.

"I can play the keyboard," Carlos said. "I have a little portable one."

"We should do it!" Cooper said. "That would be so cool. We'd rock the place."

Rhino nodded. "Think about it, Carlos. It could be a lot of fun!"

Carlos shrugged. "Maybe," he muttered.

The idea sounded great to Rhino. He had another idea, too. His thinker told him not to do it, but he blurted it out anyway. "A rock band needs a guitarist," he said. "I'm the man for that." He held his baseball bat like a guitar and pretended to strum it.

"You play the guitar?" Carlos asked.

"Sure," Rhino replied. He pictured himself on a stage in front of a large audience, rocking out with a hot guitar solo. All the fans were on their feet, dancing to the music.

"Wait," Cooper said, looking puzzled. "Since when do you play the guitar, Rhino?"

"I've been playing for a while."

"Really?" Cooper asked.

Rhino's voice sounded a little less sure this time. "Yeah?" *Uh-oh. What am I saying?* Rhino's thinker chimed in.

"You and I hang out together every day," Cooper said. "I've never seen you play the guitar."

Rhino looked away and his palms started to feel sweaty. "C.J.'s been teaching me. At night."

That was somewhat true. Rhino's older brother had been taking guitar lessons for a couple of months, and he'd shown Rhino how to play a few chords. But C.J. was no expert, and Rhino definitely wasn't either.

Rhino had recently begun taking trombone lessons, so he was familiar with reading musical notes and he had a good sense of timing. When C.J. started taking lessons, Rhino remembered his brother saying that every band needs a guitarist. That's why Rhino had jumped at the opportunity when Cooper and Carlos were talking about performing at the talent show, but Rhino knew that he shouldn't have said he could play the guitar. There was no way he was ready to perform in a band.

Still, the idea seemed very cool. And the talent

show was two weeks away. If Rhino practiced every night, maybe he would be good enough by then.

Carlos slapped hands with Cooper. "I'll do it," he said. "We'll sign up for the talent show tomorrow at school. What will we call ourselves?"

"Mustang Rock!" Cooper said. "Starring Carlos Rivera."

Carlos blushed. "I was just trying to practice for Sunday's church service," he said softly. "I didn't expect to be discovered by a talent agent like Cooper."

"Speaking of practice, there's no time to waste," Cooper said. "How about Saturday after our game? We can practice at my house, since my drums are set up there."

"Sounds great," Rhino said. He gulped. What was he getting himself into?

"Should be interesting," Cooper said, smirking at Rhino. "We uncovered Carlos's hidden singing talent today. Guess we'll see your hidden guitar talent on Saturday afternoon."

Coach Ray called the players onto the field. The practice session was nearly over, but there was still time to work on fielding. Rhino grabbed his glove and hurried to first base.

I'm in a big mess now, Rhino's thinker told him. *Cooper's suspicious, and he has a good reason to be. I only have two days to learn how to play the guitar!*

· CHAPTER 2 ·
Ready to Rock

Rhino rushed into the house. He wanted to see if he remembered any of the guitar chords C.J. had shown him.

"Hi, Grandpa!" he called as he ran up the stairs. "I'll be right down."

"Wash up," Grandpa James called. "Dinner's almost ready."

Rhino poked his head into C.J.'s room, but his brother wasn't there. Rhino carefully picked up the guitar. He set his fingers in position to play a chord, just as C.J. had shown him. Then he strummed the strings a few times.

Not bad, Rhino thought. *If I can learn three or four more chords, I might be all right.*

Rhino changed out of his baseball gear and washed his hands. He eyed his small alto trombone. Rhino knew more about playing that instrument, even though he'd only had three lessons. He played a few notes, then went downstairs.

C.J. was setting the table. The two brothers looked a lot alike, but C.J. was taller and had more muscle than Rhino.

Rhino took the milk carton from the refrigerator and filled three glasses.

"Sounded like a symphony up there for a few seconds," Grandpa James said with a smile. "Glad to hear you practicing."

"Was that my guitar I heard?" C.J. asked.

"Just one chord," Rhino said. "Can you teach me more after dinner?"

"Hold on," Grandpa said. "You just started learning the trombone, Little Rhino. I think you should concentrate on that."

Rhino nodded. "I will. But I'd like to learn to play the guitar. A little. In a hurry. Just enough to help somebody out."

Grandpa set a steaming bowl of macaroni and cheese on the table. He squinted at Rhino. "How would learning the guitar help someone out?" he asked.

Rhino scooped some lettuce and tomatoes onto his plate and squirmed. "You know Carlos, from my team? He's an awesome singer. But he's shy. He wants to enter the school talent show, but he needs some support. Cooper can drum for him . . ."

"And you can told him you can play the guitar?" C.J. asked. "Every band does need a guitar player . . ."

Rhino shrugged. "I've got two weeks to learn."

C.J. laughed. "I'm sure you'll be a pro by then! You'll be rocking and rolling and jamming."

Grandpa cleared his throat and raised his bushy eyebrows. "Sounds like you boxed yourself into a corner. What do you plan to do about it?"

Rhino's thinker told him he should call Cooper and Carlos and admit that he wasn't ready to be in a band. But he really wanted to perform. "Can't I learn enough in two weeks?" he asked.

"I can show you some more chords, but I've only had a few lessons myself," C.J. said. "There's no way I would join a band yet."

Grandpa rubbed his chin. "Did Carlos choose a song?"

Rhino shook his head. "It would have to be something easy to play. I figure that I can keep up with the melody if it's just a few simple notes."

"You're supposed to practice the trombone for an hour a day," Grandpa said. "Plus there's school-work, baseball, and chores. You don't have much extra time."

Rhino set down his fork. "I could get up early."

"Hold on," C.J. said. "Nobody will be able to sleep through an early-morning jam session."

Rhino frowned. He felt certain that he could learn quickly enough to play something.

"Here's what you can try," Grandpa said. "Half an hour of trombone every evening, and half an hour of guitar. If you find some extra time, you can put in a little more guitar practice. We'll give it a week. If you're not playing well enough by then, you'll have to tell your friends. It wouldn't be fair to Carlos."

Rhino lifted a forkful of food into his mouth. "I'll start tonight," he said. "Thanks, Grandpa!"

"We'll see," Grandpa replied. "Homework first."

"I know."

Books were always first in Grandpa James's house. On days like today, when baseball practice was right after school, homework could wait until after dinner. Rhino and C.J. worked hard at their schoolwork so they could enjoy other things like sports. Taking on another activity like playing the guitar would require some extra hard work.

I'm ready for this, Rhino thought. *I hope.* He scooped up some mac and cheese and shut his eyes, enjoying the smell. He saw himself strutting with the guitar while Cooper banged the drums and Carlos belted out a song.

"Can we listen to some of your music collection later?" Rhino asked Grandpa. "Those old songs, like the Jackson 5 or the Supremes. What do you call that style?"

"Motown," Grandpa said with a smile. "You think you can handle that? Pretty cool stuff."

"Carlos is a *great* singer," Rhino said. "But I think he'll want to sing something a little more modern than Motown. If we can get his confidence up, he'll rock!"

C.J. laughed again. "I don't think Carlos is the problem. But he'll need a real guitarist backing him up. You'd better find a *lot* of spare time in the next couple of weeks."

Rhino nodded and took another bite of dinner. He'd learned so much lately because he'd set his mind to doing it. Playing first base for the Mustangs meant learning all sorts of baseball skills he'd never imagined. Things like proper footwork for positioning himself on the base, and how to handle a bouncing throw from another infielder.

I learned all that by sticking to it, even when I struggled a few times, his thinker told him. *I can apply that same effort to learning the guitar.*

Rhino thought about one of his favorite songs. He tapped his foot and pictured himself jamming on the stage again. He could see it. He could believe it.

But, like hitting a home run or making a diving catch, it wouldn't come easy. There was a lot of hard work ahead.

And not much time at all. *Stay committed and always try my best.*

· CHAPTER 3 ·
Convincing Carlos

Rhino unwrapped his peanut-butter-and-jelly sandwich. He looked around the cafeteria and saw Carlos in the corner.

Rhino always ate lunch with a group of his friends so that they could talk about fun things— like dinosaurs and astronomy. But today Rhino had some business to take care of first.

"Hey, Carlos," Rhino said. "Let me join you."

Carlos pulled his tray closer to him and smiled. Rhino had never noticed Carlos without his Mustangs cap. His hair was cut very short, so his ears seemed to stick out.

"Should we sign up for the talent show after lunch?" Rhino asked. "We can leave the cafeteria a few minutes early and sign up at the principal's office."

Carlos looked down at his tray and winced. "Well," he said. "I don't know."

"What's wrong?" Rhino asked. "It'll be great."

Carlos tapped his fingers on the table. "I've never sung in public." *And I don't actually play the guitar,* Rhino's thinker said.

"But you sing in church every week, right?" Rhino was surprised that Carlos seemed unsure of himself again. Hadn't he and Cooper convinced him yesterday?

"Church is different," Carlos said. "I'm with a big choir, so no one's looking just at me."

Wow, he's very shy, Rhino thought.

"I practiced for two hours last night," Rhino said. C.J. had shown him two new chords. Rhino's fingertips were sore from the extra practice. "There are a lot of cool songs we could perform."

"Maybe," Carlos said. "I wish I was confident like you."

"I'm not so confident," Rhino said. "Not at everything. But I'm confident at the things I'm good at and enjoy doing, like hitting a baseball or talking about dinosaurs. And you're *great* at singing, so you should be confident about that."

"I love singing," Carlos replied. "But being on stage, with every kid in the school watching me? I wouldn't love that."

"You never know," Rhino said.

Carlos shook his head. "It's like baseball," he said. "When I get up to bat, I'm scared stiff. Not that I'll strike out or get hit by a pitch, but just because everyone's watching. That makes me nervous. Singing a solo would be even worse!"

Rhino had to think about that. He loved being at bat, especially when the game was on the line. Hitting a home run to win a game was a great feeling. He looked forward to it every chance he got.

"Let's sign up," Rhino said. "Then we'll practice.

If you decide you don't want to perform, then we can drop out. But let's give it a try, okay?"

"I guess so," Carlos said weakly.

"Remember, Cooper and I will be up there on the stage with you."

"I know," Carlos said. "But I'll be the one singing."

"Exactly," Rhino said. "With your great voice!"

Carlos laughed. "All right," he said. "You can go to the dinosaur table."

"I'll be back in plenty of time," Rhino said. "Don't leave the cafeteria without me."

Rhino should have invited Carlos to join the dinosaur discussion, but he knew Carlos would rather not. *Maybe soon,* his thinker told him. *After you give his confidence another boost!*

Rhino took a seat between Cooper and their friend Bella. She played right field for the Mustangs, and her father was the coach of the team.

"What was that about?" Bella asked. "Baseball strategy?"

"Talent show strategy," Rhino said.

Bella's eyes opened wide. "Are you entering?" she asked. "My dance team is. We have a very cool routine."

"We've got a band," Rhino said.

"Wow!" Bella shook her dark ponytail and grinned.

Cooper leaned forward so he could see Bella. "We *might* have a band," he said. "Depends on our mystery guitar player."

"Carlos?"

"No," Cooper said. "Carlos is the singer. Rhino claims to be a guitar hero."

"I never knew that," Bella replied happily.

"Neither did I," Cooper said.

Rhino took a bite of his sandwich. He'd been happy with the way his practicing had gone the night before, but he had a long way to go before he could play a song. *If you keep at it, you'll be able to play,* his thinker told him. But he wasn't sure if he believed it. Maybe he was *too* confident.

"So Carlos is a singer, huh?" Bella said. "I never would have guessed that. He's so quiet. I haven't heard him say ten words all season."

Other kids at the table started talking about the talent show, too. Kerry said she would be playing a violin solo. Ariana was on the dance team with Bella. A boy with round glasses and spiky red hair said, "Wait until you see my magic act."

Within a few minutes, Rhino realized there would be no dinosaur discussion today. He finished his BBQ chips and the last swallow of milk, then nudged Cooper. "Let's get Carlos and sign up."

Carlos didn't say a word as they filled out the sign-up sheet at the principal's office. Rhino wrote *Mustang Rock* and *band* for the name and type of act, and he listed their three names.

"What should I write for 'length of act'?" he asked.

"Three minutes," Cooper said. "That's how long most of those songs are."

"That's our next job," Rhino said. "Choosing a song."

"We'll work on a few on Saturday afternoon," Cooper said.

Carlos waved his hand and headed toward his classroom. "See you at tomorrow's game," he said.

Rhino watched Carlos go, then turned toward his own classroom. "Should we be worried about him?" Rhino asked. "I'm not so sure he can face the pressure. Hope he doesn't back out on us."

Cooper shrugged. "It isn't him I'm concerned about," he said. "Carlos has talent. I *know* what he can do."

Rhino scowled. What was Cooper saying? Rhino had practiced a lot last night! And he planned to continue every night until the talent show. "I'll be ready," he said softly.

"We'll see tomorrow," Cooper replied.

Rhino gulped. Saturday's band practice might be tougher than any baseball game he'd ever played!

· CHAPTER 4 ·
Bouncing Back?

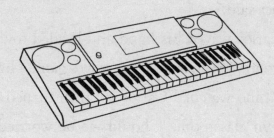

Two outs!" Rhino called, holding up his index finger. He made eye contact with each of the other infielders. As the first baseman, Rhino felt responsible for keeping his teammates alert.

The Mustangs were clinging to a one-run lead over the Wolves, who were on their last at bat. One more out would seal the win for Rhino's team, but the Wolves had a runner on first base.

Rhino bounced on his toes. "Strike him out, Dylan," he called to the pitcher.

Or let him hit it here, he thought. *I'll catch anything that comes my way.*

The batter was a lefty, like Rhino, and he'd hit the ball hard in both of his at bats today.

"Strike one!" called the umpire as the batter took a powerful swing.

Rhino glanced at Carlos, who was playing second base. Carlos took a half step back, closer to the outfield.

The batter lined the next pitch deep over Rhino's head, but it was definitely foul.

"No batter!" yelled the infielders. "Finish this off, Dylan."

The batter made good contact on the next pitch, driving a sizzling ground ball to the left of second base. Carlos stabbed at it and stopped the roll, but the ball bounced away and he had to chase it. The batter easily made it to first base and the other runner slid into second.

Carlos tossed the ball to Dylan and kicked at the dirt.

"Tough play," Rhino called. "Good hustle, Carlos!"

Carlos shook his head. "Bad error," he said.

"Get the next one," Rhino said. "Two outs!"

The next batter hit the ball in the same direction, but closer to Rhino. Rhino hesitated for a split second. Would Carlos get to it? But Rhino had the better shot. He sprinted and lunged, nabbing the ball as it reached the edge of the outfield grass. Dylan was running to cover first base, but the play would be close.

Rhino was off balance. His throw rocketed over Dylan's head and bounced off the dugout fence. The catcher raced to pick it up, but that left no one to cover home. The runner from second scored easily, and the game was tied.

"Settle down out there, guys!" called Coach Ray.

Dylan glared at Rhino. "Nice throw," he said. "If I was ten feet tall!"

Rhino ignored him. Dylan was always blaming others when things didn't go right.

"Nice try, Rhino," Carlos said. "Get the next one."

Rhino did. The next batter hit a soft pop fly that Rhino caught in foul territory to end the inning.

Make up for that error, his thinker told him. He wouldn't have to wait long. Rhino would be leading off the bottom of the inning.

He picked up his bat and took a few quick cuts.

"One big swing," Bella called from the dugout. "End this game with a homer, Rhino."

Rhino knew he needed to wait for a good pitch and not swing at a bad one. But the first pitch was fast and waist high, right in his zone. He blasted it down the line and took off.

As Rhino rounded first base he could see the right fielder chasing the ball, and he knew he'd get at least a double.

Rhino reached second and heard Coach Ray yelling to go for third. He sprinted harder.

"Slide!" Bella shouted.

A cloud of dirt sprayed up as Rhino slid cleanly into the base.

All the Mustangs were standing and yelling. Manny, the left fielder, stepped into the batter's box. A fly ball into the outfield would bring Rhino home with the winning run.

Rhino took a deep breath and clapped his hands.

Manny lined the first pitch up the middle.

Rhino stomped hard on home plate as he scored the game winner. His teammates swarmed him, laughing and cheering.

It was a wonderful feeling.

"Way to come through, Rhino," Carlos said. "I'm glad I didn't have to bat right after making an error."

"That error fired me up," Rhino said.

"You're that confident even after a mistake?" Carlos said. "Wish I was like that."

Cooper patted Carlos on the shoulder. "Speaking of confidence, are you ready to rock?"

Carlos looked terrified. "Here?"

Cooper laughed. "At my house."

Rhino suddenly felt his sweat turn cold. Band practice. He wasn't ready for that.

C.J. had patiently worked with Rhino the night before, and Rhino made some progress with the chords. But he couldn't string two notes together smoothly. He had to think about where to place his fingers after each one. It wasn't easy.

Rhino took a seat on the dugout bench and reached for his ankle. He winced and made a loud "Oo-uu-ch."

Cooper gave him a look of surprise.

"I think I hurt my ankle sliding into third," Rhino said. He'd missed a couple of games early in the season with a sprained ankle, so he needed to be careful. His teammates knew that.

"It looked okay when you were running toward home plate," Cooper said.

"Maybe that's when I hurt it," Rhino said. He gently rubbed the ankle. "It's sore! I should probably go home and ice it."

"Maybe we should get an ambulance," Cooper said sarcastically.

"I'll walk," Rhino mumbled. "It'll be good for it."

"But no band practice, right?" Cooper said.

"Maybe later."

Cooper nodded and frowned. "I thought so," he said, turning toward Carlos. "We're a duet today. Probably for the talent show, too."

"Look, I hurt my ankle, okay?" Rhino said sharply. "I couldn't help it. We'll still have plenty of time to practice. I'll be ready for the show."

"But not today," Cooper said. "Come on, Carlos."

Carlos stared at Rhino. "Great game today," he said. "Thanks for being supportive when I made that error."

Rhino gave him a tight smile. "We always bounce back," he said. "Have a good jam session. I promise I'll be at the next one."

Carlos brightened. "Yeah. Go ice that ankle. I need you in my band!"

Rhino sat in the dugout for several minutes. Everyone else was gone. When he stood up, he tested his foot. It felt fine. He knew it would.

I'd better spend all afternoon on the guitar, Rhino thought. *All the confidence in the world won't help if I don't have the skills to back it up.*

· CHAPTER 5 ·
Sour Notes

Rhino felt guilty as he walked slowly toward home. *It isn't like you to lie,* his thinker told him.

He'd been brave early in the season when Dylan tried to bully him. And he'd faced up to a tough situation when Coach Ray had switched him from the outfield to first base. Those things made him proud.

Lying about his ankle did not.

He didn't give Grandpa James his usual happy greeting. Just "hi."

"I take it that the Mustangs lost?" Grandpa asked.

"No. We won. I hit a triple and broke a tie in the last inning."

Grandpa put his hand on Rhino's shoulder. "You don't look very happy."

Rhino stared at his shoes. "We were supposed to practice for the band this afternoon."

"Somebody cancelled?" Grandpa asked.

"I did." Rhino looked up and met Grandpa's gaze. "I'm just not ready yet."

"Then you need to practice," Grandpa replied.

"I know. But I'm *really* not ready. I will be, but I didn't want Cooper and Carlos to see what a beginner I am."

Rhino practiced playing the guitar for nearly an hour after lunch. But he was restless. He knew that running or jumping or playing any sport usually calmed him down, so he went out to the backyard to hit some baseballs.

Grandpa had built a batting cage in the yard for

Rhino and C.J. The black netting kept the hit balls from leaving the yard.

Rhino set a ball on a tee and swung hard. The ball took off with a satisfying *smack* and sailed into the net.

Rhino hit the ball fifty times, but he still had a lot of energy. He picked up his mitt and left the cage, tossing a ball high into the air. He ran under it and made the catch.

This time he threw it even higher. The ball drifted toward the hedges, and Rhino ran toward it. He leaned against the hedge and stretched his arm, imagining that he was saving a home run with a leaping grab.

"Looks like you've recovered," came a voice from the driveway. Cooper was standing with his hands on his hips. His shaggy hair stuck out from under his Mustangs cap.

Rhino just stared back.

"Look," Cooper said. "You're either ready to be

part of Mustang Rock or you're not. Carlos and I can manage without you if you want to back out."

"I don't want out," Rhino said.

"Show me what you can do," Cooper said. "I'm not trying to give you a hard time, but I need to see for myself."

Rhino led Cooper up to C.J.'s room. C.J. had said Rhino could use the guitar anytime. In fact, C.J. had expected Rhino to take it to Cooper's house today for practice.

"Here's C," Rhino said, setting his fingers and strumming a basic chord.

Cooper nodded, "Okay."

"And G," Rhino said, shifting his fingers. He stopped to think for a second, then strummed again. "Now A."

"All right, so you know some of the basics," Cooper said. "But one chord at a time is not a song."

"I know."

"*Can* you play a song?" Cooper asked.

Rhino carefully held on to the guitar. "Not yet."

"Well, Carlos and I sounded good without you," Cooper said. "So if you can keep up with a few chords, you probably won't hurt us. But you need to practice with us. Monday after school. No excuses."

"I have to do my homework first."

"Then right after homework."

Rhino played the three chords again. He tried to switch from chord to chord as quickly as he could, but it wasn't easy.

"Did you decide on a song for the talent show?" Rhino asked.

"I think so." Cooper sat on the edge of the bed. "We tried a few slow ones to warm up, and then we got rolling. Carlos finally relaxed, and he rocked. But that was without an audience, of course. That's why we need you."

"Why?"

"Because Carlos feels more positive when you're around," Cooper said. "He knows you won't make fun of him, or let anyone else do it."

"That's true." Rhino stuck up for all his friends and teammates. He knew that he was the team leader and always wanted to act like it.

"Play those three chords again," Cooper said. "Like this: G . . . A . . . C . . . G. A. C." He stretched his fingers and slowly tapped a beat on the edge of C.J.'s desk. *Bop . . . bop . . . BOP . . . Bop. Bop. BOP.*

Rhino struggled to keep up at first, but it got easier after a few minutes.

"Good!" Cooper said. He kept tapping, a little faster now. *Bop-bop-BOP. Bop-bop-BOP.*

Rhino kept repeating the chords. G-A-C. G-A-C. He grinned. It was still pretty slow, but it sounded a *little* like a song.

"You're rocking!" Cooper said. "You might be all right yet, Rhino. With those three chords, plus a few D's and E's, you could play a song like 'Upside Down, Inside Out.'"

"That new song?" Rhino asked.

"Yeah. Carlos was belting that out this afternoon. Cool, huh?"

Rhino knew the song well. C.J. listened to it all the time. "But it's a lot faster than what we were just playing, isn't it?"

"Much faster," Cooper said. "And more complicated."

Rhino wasn't sure he could do that.

Grandpa James looked into the room. "You two are cooking," he said. "Cooper, you ought to be a teacher. Little Rhino sounded like a pro!"

Rhino laughed. "Not quite. But that *was* a good lesson. Can't wait for Monday's band practice."

"Speaking of practice, would it be all right if I hit a few baseballs in the batting cage?" Cooper asked. "I struck out twice today. My timing is good for drumming, but it was way off for hitting."

"Let's go!" Rhino said. As they hurried down the stairs, Rhino's thinker told him to add something else.

"Thanks for being a good friend, Cooper," he said. "You keep me on my toes. I can't fool you about *anything*."

Rhino felt so much happier that Cooper knew the truth. He should have been honest from the start.

· CHAPTER 6 ·
Changing Pace

Rhino was surprised to see Bella and Ariana when he arrived at Cooper's house after school on Monday. The girls looked like they were in their dance-team outfits. They must have just been practicing their routine.

"Cooper said we could watch you guys practice," Bella said. "He said Carlos is amazing. I hope we don't make him nervous."

You're making me *nervous,* Rhino thought. He didn't want anyone watching his first session with the band. *But I'll be in front of an audience soon,* his thinker said. *I might as well get used to it.*

They were right about Carlos. He blushed when he saw the girls and mumbled that his throat might be too dry for singing today.

"Let's start with an easy one," Cooper said. "We'll play 'Overtime Run.' Nice and slow, right, Rhino?"

Cooper handed Rhino a sheet with the lyrics and the chords. Rhino set his fingers for the first chord. The song was mostly E's and A's. It looked easy.

"Okay?" Cooper asked him.

Rhino nodded.

They plodded through the song, and Rhino made only a few mistakes. Carlos sang so softly that his keyboard drowned out his voice.

"Nice," Bella said when the song ended.

Rhino knew better. A performance like that would be an embarrassment at the talent show. They'd never win.

"You have a great voice, Carlos," Bella said. "But we need to hear it more. It sounds better than any instrument, so speak up!"

Carlos looked down at the keyboard, but he was holding back a smile. He seemed less afraid when he looked up.

"Let's try it again," Cooper said. "A little quicker."

They ran through the song three more times. Rhino winced with every mistake he made, but the others said he sounded pretty good.

"Carlos's voice and keyboard should be what we hear the most," Ariana said. "The guitar is more in the background."

Bella laughed. "Better keep it that way." She nudged Ariana and stood. "Time to go," she said. "Thanks for letting us watch. You'll be great." She winked at Rhino and headed for the door.

"Not bad for a warm-up," Cooper said. He banged the drums a few times. "But 'Upside Down, Inside Out' is a lot faster and more complex. We need to play a lively song like that to win the talent show."

Rhino turned to the sheet music for that song. It was mostly G's and C's and A's, but the pattern changed back and forth several times.

Rhino hit more sour notes than good ones.

"That was a total flop," Cooper said after the first time through.

Rhino knew that was his fault. He could play all the chords, but the rapid pace made it very hard for him to keep up.

"Listen to me and Carlos one time," Cooper said. "Imagine that you're playing the chords with us, but don't try to play along yet."

I don't see how that will help, Rhino thought. But then he remembered that thinking about hitting a baseball *did* help when the time came to do it in a game. Maybe Cooper's idea was the same. Rhino could think about changing from G to A to C much more quickly than he could actually move his fingers into position.

He joined in the next time Carlos and Cooper

started the song. They played it five more times. Carlos sounded great.

Rhino didn't.

"Keep at it," Cooper said as Rhino put the guitar in its case. "Practice tonight at home. We can have another session on Wednesday, and after the game on Saturday."

Rhino and Carlos left together. Carlos was still singing "Upside Down, Inside Out" very softly as they walked along the sidewalk.

"Feeling confident?" Rhino asked.

Carlos let out a deep breath. "For now," he said. "I love that song. When I forget that anyone's watching, it's easy." Carlos shook his head. "But how will I ever forget when an entire audience is staring at me?"

"It's hard," Rhino said. "But you nailed that song today. You made it *yours*. I'm sorry I kept messing up and holding you back."

"We'll keep practicing," Carlos said. "You'll get better."

"I hope so. You deserve it."

They reached Carlos's street and he turned toward home. Rhino walked the next few blocks alone.

He'd made some progress today, but he was nowhere close to playing that song. Carlos and Cooper played their instruments without even thinking. Would it become like that for him?

"Rhino!" came a shout. C.J. was waving to him from a block away. He was in his school baseball uniform. He ran to catch up to Rhino.

C.J. patted Rhino on the shoulder. "We won," he said. "Tough game. Their pitcher had us shut out for five innings, but then we rallied. How'd the session go?"

Rhino thought for a few seconds. "All right," he said. "It was fun, but . . ."

C.J. smiled. "Over your head?"

"Way over."

"But fun anyway?" C.J. asked.

"Yeah." It *had* been fun, despite Rhino's struggles.

"Fun is good," C.J. said. "We put so much pressure on ourselves sometimes, you know? Like today. I was so nervous when I batted the last time. The whole game was riding on my shoulders."

"And what happened?"

"Clean single. I drove in the winning run."

Rhino smiled. "Sometimes the fun comes later. After you get the hit."

"Right," C.J. said. "Being calm works better than being nervous. But no matter how many times we tell ourselves that, the nerves kick in."

They'd reached their house. Being home with Grandpa James was always the best place to be.

"Let's go," C.J. said. "I smell Grandpa's famous pasta sauce, and I'm starving!"

They hurried into the house. Rhino felt hungry, too. He needed a good meal, because tonight he'd be playing the guitar until bedtime. He wanted to practice every spare minute until the show.

CHAPTER 7

Imagine That!

The afternoon was warm and sunny. Baseball weather! Rhino took a deep breath and smelled the freshly cut grass on the infield. He loved practice almost as much as the games. He'd been playing first base for nearly an hour, and he was eager to bat.

Crack! The batter hit the ball and Rhino darted toward first base. Carlos fielded a short hop and tossed the ball to Rhino, putting the batter out.

"Good job, Carlos," Rhino said. He threw the ball back to Coach Ray.

"Infielders up!" Coach called.

It was their turn to hit!

Rhino high-fived his teammate Paul, who would play first base while Rhino took batting practice.

Rhino joined Cooper, Carlos, and Dylan in the dugout. He pointed to Cooper and said, "You can bat first."

"Yeah," Dylan said. "You need the most practice, Cooper. I got dizzy watching you swing and miss so many times in the last game."

Dylan was always teasing someone. At least he wasn't as nasty about it as he used to be. "I heard that you guys think you're rock stars," he said.

Rhino caught Carlos's eye and gave him a half smile. "One of us is pretty good," he said. "You'll see."

"What a joke," Dylan said. "I can't wait to see you guys mess up in the talent show. Squeaky-voiced Carlos will have everybody laughing. Or running for the doors."

"At least we're out there trying," Rhino said. "What's your talent, Dylan? Making enemies?"

Dylan laughed. "My talent is hitting home runs," he said. He picked up a bat and headed for the on-deck circle. "Watch and learn."

Carlos sighed. "That's what I don't like about performing," he said. "Too many people like that to make fun of me."

"There's only one Dylan," Rhino said. "Everybody else wants you to do well. He's just mad because he can't sing the way you can."

Rhino batted after Dylan. With ten swings, he hit three pitches over the fence and four more deep into the outfield. The sweat felt good trickling down his back. His arms were strong and his vision was clear.

"Nice at bat," Carlos said as Rhino passed him in the on-deck circle. "I guess it's my turn. You're a tough act to follow."

"Relax," Rhino said. "Just meet the ball."

But Carlos struggled. Six of his swings missed completely. He managed three weak grounders and a pop out.

"Dylan shook me up," Carlos whispered as he rejoined Rhino in the dugout.

"That's what he does," Rhino said. "You have to ignore him when he's like that."

"Easy for you to say." Carlos leaned over and tightened the laces of his cleats. "I couldn't hit at all today. I knew he'd start making fun of me if I didn't hit well, so I was swinging way too hard."

Rhino had learned that trying too hard could be just as bad as not trying hard enough. But he had a good tip for Carlos. It was something he'd learned after struggling to hit early in the season. "Do you ever go out into your yard and just swing the bat?" he asked.

"Sure," Carlos said. "I do it all the time. And I throw baseballs high into the air and catch them, or I bounce a ball off a wall and field it."

That was exactly what Rhino liked to do. "I'll bet that you imagine yourself doing great things," he said. "Hitting a home run or making a diving catch."

"Yeah. Doesn't everybody?"

"I know I do," Rhino said. "The thing is, you have to be that relaxed and confident in a game, too. It's not so different. The bat is the same. The fly balls drop at the same speed, right? And those rebounds off the wall are usually *harder* to field than a batted grounder."

"That's probably true," Carlos said. His eyes were wide, taking in everything Rhino said.

"So forget that anyone's watching," Rhino added. "Just do the same things you do when you're alone. Being afraid that you'll strike out or drop the ball doesn't help. Listening to someone like Dylan is a waste of time."

Carlos nodded. "Like when I'm singing. I never get nervous singing alone, in my room. And I don't feel nervous about practicing with Cooper anymore. But I still get *very* nervous every time I think about the talent show."

"But that doesn't help, right?"

"I guess not," Carlos said. But he didn't sound convinced.

As the next batters came in from the outfield, Rhino picked up his glove and headed for first base again. He had a lot of energy, and all those big hits he'd made had him excited. He couldn't wait for the Mustangs' next game. *That's what I call a talent show,* he thought. He wished he could hit baseballs on the stage instead of trying to play the guitar. *First place,* he thought. *Best hitter.* That would be much easier than playing those chords.

Bella was at bat. Rhino smacked his glove with his bare hand and bounced on his toes. "Strike her out!" he joked. Coach Ray wouldn't want to strike out his own daughter.

Bella hit a zinger that soared over Rhino's head and dropped into right field. She pointed the bat at him and smiled. Rhino laughed.

Rhino looked around the field. He felt so lucky

to be on this team with his best friend, Cooper. He'd learned a lot from Coach Ray about baseball and about being a helpful teammate. And he'd made some good new friends in Bella and Carlos.

Baseball sure was fun.

· CHAPTER 8 ·
Panic!

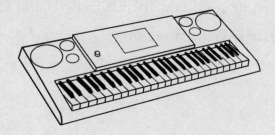

The week went by fast. The Mustangs won their game on Saturday, and Rhino hit a home run and a double. Carlos gained more confidence every time the band practiced.

But Rhino's guitar playing hadn't improved enough.

He did fine when they warmed up with a slower song like "Overtime Run." But the faster song they planned to play in the show gave Rhino a lot of trouble. Three more sessions with the band and many hours at home made him only a little better at it. As soon as the music sped up, Rhino tripped over some of the chords.

Thursday morning at breakfast, Rhino was quieter than usual. The talent show was that night. How did it get here so quickly?

"You're deep in thought, Little Rhino," Grandpa James said. "What's on your mind?"

"His big moment!" C.J. said. "The debut of the band."

Rhino glared at C.J. "I can speak for myself," he said.

C.J. gave Rhino a light tap on the arm. "Relax," he said. There was that word again.

"Sorry," Rhino said. "I didn't mean to snap at you."

Rhino took a bite of toast. He was excited about the show, but he wasn't sure how it would go. He'd stayed up late last night thinking about it.

"I'm still going over the notes in my head," Rhino said. "Getting ready."

"You're as ready as you're going to be," Grandpa said. "Just enjoy the show. I can't wait."

Rhino could wait. Being "as ready as you're going to be" didn't sound good. He *wasn't* ready. Mustang Rock would have one more chance to practice at school this morning, but only for a few minutes.

"Remember one thing," Grandpa said. "The talent show is supposed to be fun. You have a whole day at school, so don't waste time worrying about tonight. Concentrate on your schoolwork."

"I will," Rhino replied. But he knew that wouldn't be easy.

At school, Mrs. Imburgia explained how most of Earth's energy comes from the sun. Rhino knew that already, but anything about the solar system interested him.

Later, he worked on math problems. Every few minutes he looked up at the clock. *Move faster,* he thought.

As soon as the classroom bell rang at ten a.m., Cooper turned to Rhino with a serious look. "This is it," he said. "Our last chance to get it right."

Rhino gulped. Anyone entered in the talent show was allowed a short practice session today instead of going to recess, and Mustang Rock was taking advantage of that. Rhino and Cooper hurried to the auditorium to meet Carlos. This would be their final session.

There was no time to spare. Instead of warming up with a slower song, they started in on "Upside Down, Inside Out." Cooper tapped out the rocking beat. Carlos joined in with his keyboard and Rhino on the guitar.

Rhino watched his fingers, moving them as quickly as he could to change chords. But as soon as Carlos started to sing, Cooper banged on the bass drum to get them to stop.

"Sorry," Rhino said. He'd hit two sour notes in a row.

Cooper frowned and shook his head.

"Just relax, Rhino," Carlos said. That was the same advice Rhino always gave Carlos about baseball.

"Try it again," Cooper said. "This is the real deal. We have to play it all the way through at the right pace."

Rhino couldn't keep up. He'd practiced so hard for this, but he just wasn't ready for the faster song.

"I should drop out of the band," Rhino said. "You two can play without me. I'm holding you back."

"No way!" Carlos said. He sounded scared. "Look, let's play 'Overtime Run' first."

"That won't help!" Cooper said. "We only have a few minutes left to practice."

"It's okay," Carlos said calmly. "Rhino plays better when he's had a chance to warm up with something slower. It gets us into a groove. We'll do the faster song later."

Rhino let out his breath. He didn't want to drop out, but he also didn't want to mess up Carlos's performance.

They ran through the slower song. Carlos's voice was strong and clear.

"Once more," Carlos said as the song ended.

"We're running out of time," Cooper said firmly. "We have to be back in class in five minutes."

"It's all right," Carlos said. "Let's play 'Overtime Run' one more time. Just a little faster than usual."

Cooper shook his head with more force. "We need to do the other one," he said. But he started the beat for "Overtime Run" anyway.

Rhino kept up with the slightly faster pace, but this song was easy. He kept thinking about how foolish he'd look as he messed up "Upside Down, Inside Out" on the stage. But he also noticed how calm Carlos seemed all of a sudden.

The bell rang seconds after they finished.

"We're in trouble," Cooper said. "We didn't even practice 'Upside Down, Inside Out!'"

"Don't worry," Carlos said. He nodded to Rhino and whispered. "We're ready for the show. I promise."

Rhino felt a cold sweat run down his neck. He wasn't ready, and he knew it.

Cooper was mumbling about how they had wasted the entire practice session. But Carlos was relaxed. He was even smiling. Sure, he'd sung very well. Carlos was definitely ready. But Carlos also insisted that Rhino would be part of the band tonight no matter what.

Rhino followed Cooper back to their classroom. *Carlos thinks I'm ready,* Rhino thought. *Who is he trying to kid?*

One thought kept coming back to Rhino for the rest of the school day: Performing "Upside Down, Inside Out" was going to be a disaster!

· CHAPTER 9 ·
Mustang Surprise

Rhino put on his blue Mustangs jersey after dinner. He'd only worn it for baseball games, but tonight was special. Cooper and Carlos would be wearing their jerseys for the performance, too.

Rhino hadn't finished his chicken. That *never* happened. But his stomach was in knots as he thought about the performance.

You'll do fine, his thinker told him. But Rhino thought his thinker was wrong.

He picked up the guitar and tried the chord pattern again. When he played very slowly, he was able to do it without any mistakes. But it barely sounded like a song. Carlos would never sing that slowly.

Rhino didn't say anything on the ride over to the school. C.J. and Grandpa tried to start a conversation, but then they left Rhino alone to think.

The talent show contestants were supposed to report to the gym. They'd be told the order in which they'd perform, then take seats in the front row of the auditorium.

Rhino carried the guitar case toward the gym. He said hello to Coach Ray, who had dropped off Bella.

Rhino spotted Cooper under one of the baskets.

"This is it," Rhino said. "Where's Carlos?"

"Not here yet."

Rhino waved to Bella and Ariana. Four other dancers were stretching on the side of the gym with them.

Rhino looked straight at Cooper. "Do you think there's any chance Carlos won't show up?"

"I don't think so," Cooper said. "He definitely seemed ready this afternoon."

"I'm glad one of us is."

"Just do the best you can," Cooper said. "If you make a mistake . . . I mean, *when* you make a mistake, just forget about it and try to catch up to where we are."

"Okay," Rhino said. He went over the chords in his mind again. If this was a school test, he could write every note in the correct order.

But *playing* the chords was another story.

"We're the eleventh act on the schedule," Cooper said. "Out of fourteen. So we'll have a long wait."

Carlos came into the gym, smiling broadly.

"What's with him?" Cooper said. "All of a sudden he's Mr. Confidence."

Rhino shrugged. "That's because he knows he's good. I smile like that when I'm in the on-deck circle, waiting to bat."

"Hi, guys," Carlos said when he reached them.

"I just wanted to thank you for helping me out. There's no way I would do this without you."

Rhino laughed a little. "I hope you'll be thanking me *after* the show."

"I will," Carlos said. "This is going to be so cool."

Rhino's eyes met Cooper's, and they both winced.

"I don't want to ruin your mood, Carlos," Cooper said, "but why are you so confident? We couldn't get through 'Upside Down, Inside Out' even one time today. We've *never* played it without a bunch of mistakes. Do you have some kind of magic wand that's going to fix everything?"

"I have a plan," Carlos said.

"Well, let's hear it," Cooper replied. "The show starts in a few minutes."

Carlos pulled his friends closer to him, as if they were in a football huddle. "It's like this," he said.

Rhino listened carefully as Carlos explained his idea. It made a lot of sense. It might not be enough to win the talent show, but it would make things go a lot more smoothly.

Cooper nodded slowly.

Rhino grinned.

Maybe he wouldn't mess this up after all.

Rhino felt much better as he took his seat in the auditorium. He cheered loudly and let out a *whoop* when Bella and Ariana's dance team went through their lively routine.

One performer after another impressed him with their ability to sing, tell jokes, or play an instrument. To Rhino, Carlos was probably the best. But Carlos hadn't performed yet. Even with the new plan, anything could go wrong.

Before the tenth act went on, Mrs. Imburgia motioned for Mustang Rock to come backstage. They'd be next.

Mrs. Imburgia whispered to them as she looked at the list of performers. "'Upside Down, Inside Out,'" she said. "I love that song. It should be fun."

"There's a slight change," Carlos said. He pointed to the list and told the teacher what he'd decided. She said she'd be sure to announce the change when she introduced the band.

Rhino swallowed hard. *Any minute now,* he thought. *Glad I'm not the one singing.*

The audience broke into applause. The tenth act left the stage. Rhino followed Cooper out. Carlos trailed behind.

"Ladies and gentlemen, it's my pleasure to introduce Mustang Rock," Mrs. Imburgia said. "There's a change to the program. They'll be doing a different song than the one that's listed. Please enjoy 'Overtime Run.'"

Cooper tapped a drum three times, and Rhino and Carlos joined in. The pace was faster than they usually played it, but Rhino knew this easier song well. Playing it was almost automatic. He hardly had to think about changing chords.

Carlos had his eyes shut, belting out the song and even dancing as he played the keyboard. His voice was high and sweet.

Rhino could see the audience swaying and cheering. Some of the kids were standing in front of their seats and dancing.

This was great. It was almost as Rhino had first imagined it. The only difference was that Rhino wasn't trying to show off. He stayed back a few steps and just played along. This was Carlos's moment.

The audience erupted with a huge cheer as the song ended. Then people began to stand, clapping and yelling. Soon the entire audience was standing.

Rhino stepped over and gave Carlos a high five. Carlos stepped out from behind the keyboard and bowed. He had a huge grin. Rhino blinked hard.

"I always knew you'd be awesome," Rhino said.

Carlos patted Rhino's back. He was too choked up to speak.

Later, Rhino wasn't surprised when Mustang Rock was announced as the champions of the talent show. "That's all because of you," he told Carlos.

"If it wasn't for you I never would have done this," Carlos said. This time, he led the way onto the stage. The audience stood and cheered again as Mrs. Imburgia handed blue ribbons to Rhino, Carlos, and Cooper.

Grandpa James hugged Rhino after he left the stage, and C.J. raised his hand for a high five.

Bella and Ariana and other friends surrounded Carlos and told him how great he'd been. Carlos blushed, but he looked pleased.

Coach Ray said he had an idea. "Do you think Mustang Rock would do an encore performance?" he asked Rhino. "You could set up on the infield and play that song after Saturday's game."

Rhino pointed to Carlos. "I'm all for it, but you'll have to convince the star."

Carlos looked up and grinned. "Why not?" he said. "As long as I have my teammates with me, I can face anything."

Me too, Rhino thought. *On the baseball field or the stage!*

· CHAPTER 10 ·
Rocking the House

There was a lot of friendly chatter from the Sharks during Saturday's game. They'd defeated the Mustangs earlier in the season, when Rhino sat out the game with an injured ankle. Now they turned their jabbering to the Mustangs' other talents.

"That bat's too heavy!" the shortstop called when Cooper batted to lead off the game. "Use a drumstick instead."

Cooper managed a walk. He trotted to first base, kicking up a little dirt as he ran.

"He can sing but he can't hit!" yelled the third baseman when Carlos batted next.

Carlos turned the tables and smacked a line drive up the middle for a single. Cooper sailed into second, raising a bigger cloud of dirt.

Dylan struck out. Rhino stepped up to the plate. With two runners on base, he could give the Mustangs a big early lead with the right swing.

"No batter!" was the best the Sharks could come up with.

Rhino smiled. They couldn't rattle him!

The first pitch was high and outside. Rhino watched it go by. He stepped back and tapped some dirt from his cleats.

"Good eye!" Bella called from the dugout.

Rhino focused on the pitcher and waited.

This pitch looked good. Rhino made a steady swing and felt the satisfying *smack* of bat meeting ball. He sprinted toward first base, looking up as the ball soared high and deep toward the center field fence.

"That's gone!" came a cry from the bleachers.

Rhino felt a surge of energy as the ball cleared

the fence for a home run. But he didn't slow down. He raced around the bases as Cooper scored, then Carlos. Mustang Rock had given their team a 3–0 lead!

The pitcher glared at Rhino as he ran down the third baseline toward home. He punched his glove.

Then he struck out Manny and Bella to end the inning.

The Mustangs took the field. Rhino threw the ball to third base, then to Cooper, then to Carlos. His arm was loose and strong. This game could be a rout.

But the Sharks were confident. They scored a run in the second inning and two more in the third. The Mustangs' lead was gone.

Rhino led off the fourth inning. *Just meet the ball,* his thinker told him. He'd learned that he didn't have to clobber the ball every time. He had plenty of power.

The pitcher wasn't about to get burned again. He kept the ball on the edges of the strike zone. A little low. Then a little inside.

With the count at three balls and two strikes, Rhino dug in. The umpire had called a couple of strikes that Rhino didn't agree with. Another one like that and he'd strike out, so he was willing to swing at anything close.

Here came the pitch. It was high. It was outside.

Rhino connected. Again the ball took off in the air toward center field. But this time it fell short of the fence. The center fielder made the catch, and Rhino trotted back to the dugout.

The score was still tied as they entered the sixth and final inning. Carlos led off for the Mustangs, and he belted his second single of the day.

"See what a little confidence can do?" Rhino said to Cooper. "He's never had two hits in a game before."

Rhino stepped into the on-deck circle. Dylan hit a weak grounder to first base for an out, but Carlos slid safely into second.

"Give us the lead!" Cooper yelled.

This was what Rhino liked best. Game on the line. His teammates counting on him. This was *his* talent show.

Bam! Rhino lined the first pitch deep into the gap between the right fielder and center. He sprinted all the way to second base for a stand-up double.

Best of all, Carlos scored. The Mustangs had the lead.

Rhino reached third base on a grounder, but he was stranded there on the third out.

"Defense!" Rhino called as the Mustangs took the field. They'd nail down a win if they could hold the Sharks scoreless this inning.

Dylan struck out the leadoff batter.

"Here we go!" Rhino yelled. "One down!"

But Dylan was tiring. He walked the next batter and gave up a bunt single to the one after that.

Suddenly the Sharks had the tying run at second and the potential winning run on base, too.

"Any base!" Rhino called. The Mustangs could get a force-out at second or third.

He turned to Carlos and spoke a little softer. "Let's turn two," he said.

The batter fouled one off. After two balls, he popped another one over the backstop and out of play.

The cheering was loud from both sides.

Bing! The ball scooted up the middle. It looked like a hit. But Cooper darted to it and scooped it up, flipping the ball to Carlos at second base for an out. Carlos spun and fired the ball toward first.

It was a perfect throw. Rhino stretched out his glove and felt the *smack* as it arrived just ahead of the batter. Double play!

"Mustang Rock!" Rhino shouted, holding up the ball. He ran toward Carlos. They slapped hands in a leaping high five as the other Mustangs jumped and yelled.

Rhino joined his teammates as they congratulated the Sharks for a tough, close game. Then he helped Cooper and Carlos set up their instruments outside the dugout.

"Here's another double play for you!" Coach Ray called to the crowd. "The game-winning combo is also a talent show–winning band."

Cooper tapped the drums. Carlos dug into the keyboard.

This is so great, Rhino thought. He was confident and relaxed. He played every note right as Carlos knocked out his third hit of the day.

Everything was going right for Rhino.

It felt like another home run!

THE FIRST AWAY GAME!

LITTLE

Rhino

HERE'S A SNEAK PEEK AT
LITTLE RHINO #5!

Rhino! Rhino! Rhino!"

Little Rhino glanced at his teammates, who were standing inside the dugout fence, chanting his name. He nodded, but tried hard not to smile.

Rhino gripped his bat and strode to the batter's box. He took a couple of easy swings and glared at the pitcher. The pressure was on!

Bases loaded. Two outs. The Mustangs trailed by two runs in the bottom of the sixth inning. This was their last at-bat.

The Bears' pitcher squinted as he read the catcher's signals. Then he leaned forward and fired a sizzling fast ball. It looked wide, and Rhino let it go by.

"Strike!" called the umpire.

"No batter!" yelled the infielders.

"Let's go, Rhino," shouted Bella, taking a lead off second base.

Rhino tapped his bat on the plate. The crowd was on their feet, cheering.

"Ball," said the umpire as the catcher leaped high to grab the next pitch.

First place in the league was on the line in this game, and the showdown between Rhino and the pitcher was shaping up to be a classic. Rhino led the league with five home runs, and the Bears' pitcher had the best record.

Rhino had belted a two-run homer in the first inning, but he'd struck out twice since then. The Bears had played steady baseball all season. Rhino's Mustangs had come into the game on a hot streak, with five wins in a row. Whichever team won today would be alone in first place.

Rhino took a quick look at the other base runners: Carlos on third base and Dylan on first. Both were bouncing on their toes, ready to sprint.

Their teammates in the dugout chanted again. "Rhino! Rhino!"

Here came the pitch. Rhino took a massive swing.

The Bears yelled as the catcher safely caught the ball.

"Strike two!"

Rhino's thinker told him to relax. *You've been in pressure situations before. Just meet the ball.*

Rhino looked out at the scoreboard in center-field. BEARS 7, MUSTANGS 5.

He took a deep breath.

Whack! Rhino felt his muscles surge as he clobbered the next fastball. The ball streaked toward the scoreboard, but Rhino didn't watch it. He raced to first base as the crowd whooped.

Rounding first, Rhino saw the Bears' center-fielder watching helplessly as the baseball flew over his head for a home run. Rhino leaped with both hands up as he stamped on second base, then continued running.

The Mustangs won. They were in first place!

Carlos, Bella, and Dylan waited for Rhino as he ran toward home. They pounded his back and yelled as the rest of the Mustangs ran from the dugout.

"Two blasts!" shouted Bella. That was a first. Rhino had never hit two homers in one game before.

The Bears' pitcher looked glum as the teams shook hands.

"Great game," Rhino told him.

"Nice hit," the pitcher mumbled. "But we'll get you next time."

"Good luck until then," Rhino replied. "Keep that arm loose."

Coach Ray gathered the Mustangs in the dugout. "I'm very proud of this team," he said. "Winning six straight games is tough. But what I'm most proud of is your hard work and sportsmanship."

Rhino clapped and the others joined in. "Thanks, Coach," he said. "You're a great leader."

Bella nudged Rhino with her elbow and smiled.

"Winning today gives us a real honor," Coach said. "Since we're in first place, we'll be representing our league in a special tournament next weekend. It's an exhibition, so it won't affect how we're doing in this league. But it will be an exciting trip and gives us a chance to test ourselves against some very strong teams."

Wow, Rhino thought. *That sounds like a Major League honor.* He couldn't wait.

Coach told the players that he'd understand if not everyone decided to make the trip. They'd be traveling by bus to the state capital and staying overnight in a hotel. If they won their first game, they'd play in the championship game the next day.

Rhino gulped. Two nights in a hotel? Away from his brother C.J. and Grandpa James? Rhino had never slept anywhere except Grandpa James's house. Not even for a sleepover at his best friend Cooper's.

"This will be so great," Bella said to Rhino as they left the dugout.

Rhino nodded. That was easy for Bella to say. Her father would be along for the trip. Coach Ray was her dad.

Rhino felt a tap on his shoulder. He turned to see Dylan's wise-guy smile.

"Another great win, huh?" Rhino said.

Dylan shrugged. "Of course. But we'll see how well you do in the big-time tournament next weekend," he said. "Things are different at the capital. *Intense* competition."

Dylan was always trying to stir up trouble. *Just ignore him,* Rhino's thinker said. "How would you know?" Rhino asked.

"I've been in plenty of big sports events," Dylan said.

"Like what?" Rhino replied. Dylan didn't have any more experience than Rhino did. They were both playing on a real team for the first time this season.

"Too many to name," Dylan said.

"Name one."

Dylan changed the subject. "Be sure to bring your teddy bear," he said. "Being away from home overnight is going to be scary. For you."

"Why should I be scared?" Rhino asked. He *was* feeling uneasy about it. But he wasn't going to let Dylan know that.

"Believe me, you'll be afraid," Dylan said. "No big brother around. No grandfather."

Rhino started to walk away. "Get lost, Dylan. You don't know what you're talking about."

"Yeah, lay off," Cooper said, stepping over. He jutted his head toward the gate. "Let's go, Rhino."

"Great homer," Cooper said when they were out of Dylan's earshot. "And great news: My dad is going on the trip with us. You and I will room with him at the hotel."

That made Rhino feel better. Cooper's father was always kind and supportive to him.

Then Rhino had an idea. Maybe Grandpa James could be there, too! Having Grandpa along would make it the best trip ever.

Rhino felt that same surge of excitement he'd felt when he hit the game-winning homer. "State capital, here we come!"

Rhino ran all the way home. He couldn't wait to tell Grandpa James about the trip. And about his two home runs!

"Grandpa!" he called as he hurried through the back door. "Wait until you hear!"

Grandpa James caught Rhino in a bear hug and laughed. Rhino told him the news. "Cooper's dad is coming along," he said. "Can I go? Can you be there, too?"

Grandpa poured Rhino a glass of milk. "First of all, congratulations on the game," he said. "And of course you can go on the trip. You've worked very hard in baseball, and in your schoolwork. So you've earned it."

Rhino smiled. "What about you?"

Grandpa patted Rhino's shoulder. "Next Saturday evening is C.J.'s science fair," he said. "I'd love to go to your tournament, but I promised your brother weeks ago that I'd be at the fair."

"Can you drive to the tournament after?" Rhino asked.

Grandpa smiled. "I don't think so. The capital is nearly three hours away. We would get there very late at night."

Rhino rubbed his chin. "I guess I'll be okay," he said softly.

"Sure you will," Grandpa said. "But it's up to you. If you'd rather stay home, I'll understand. And so will your coach. He phoned me last night."

"He did? So you knew about the tournament before I did?"

"Of course," Grandpa said. "Coach Ray didn't want to tell the players before today's game. But he needed to make sure the parents knew. I told him I believed you'd want to play, but that it would be your decision."

Rhino stared at his glass of milk. He did want to play. And he certainly didn't want his teammates to think he was afraid to spend a night away from home. Dylan would never let him hear the end of that!

"Think it over," Grandpa James said. "But you'll need to make a firm decision by Monday. Once you decide, there will be no changing your mind."

Rhino nodded. His thinker told him to be brave. *This will be fun! And what a great chance to show your skills against the best players in the state.*

"I'm going," Rhino said firmly. "I'll be okay."

"I know you will," Grandpa said. "You've done a lot of things to be proud of this spring. This will be another one, no matter what happens in the tournament."

Rhino felt better. He finished his milk and made himself a peanut-butter-and-jelly sandwich. His favorite meal!

When C.J. came home, he and Rhino went out to the yard to have a catch. C.J. was in seventh grade—four years ahead of Rhino. He'd been playing on sports teams for several years, and was the starting shortstop for his middle-school team.

"I heard about the tournament," C.J. said. "I wish I'd had an opportunity like that when I was your age!"

"It'll be very cool," Rhino said. But he didn't sound as enthusiastic as before.

"I'm sure it will," C.J. said. "Something bothering you?"

C.J. fired a high throw and Rhino had to leap

for it. Rhino nabbed the ball, spun around, and tossed it back.

"Nice grab," C.J. said.

Rhino caught another throw. He tossed it high in the air. C.J. circled under it and made the easy catch.

"So?" C.J. asked.

Rhino shrugged. "The games don't worry me," he said. "But . . ."

"Being away from home does?"

"A little."

C.J. nodded. "I was ten the first time I did an overnighter," he said. "A year older than you are. Remember? I went camping with Devin's family."

"I think so." Rhino threw a hard grounder and C.J. scooped it up.

"I was so excited about it," C.J. said. "Fishing, hiking, cooking hot dogs over the fire. It was going to be so cool."

"Wasn't it?" Rhino caught the ball and held it. He took a few steps toward C.J.

"It was," C.J. said. "All of those things were great. We set up a couple of tents right on the shore of the lake. The moon was full that night and you could hear a million crickets chirping, and every once in a while a fish would jump. It *was* cool."

Rhino frowned. "So you weren't scared at all?"

C.J. laughed. "I didn't think I was. Then Devin and I crawled into our tent. He fell asleep in about two seconds. I just lay there, thinking about how far away I was from Grandpa James. I'd never slept in any house but this one. What if something happened? What if a bear came by, or I got lost in the woods somehow?"

"So you *were* scared."

"I was petrified." C.J. nodded toward the back steps, and he and Rhino sat down. "After about a half hour I woke Devin up. Not to tell him I was scared. I made up some excuse, like I needed a snack."

Rhino laughed. "What did he do?"

"He rolled over and went back to sleep. So I did

get a snack. I had a candy bar in my knapsack. That helped for a minute."

Rhino's thinker told him to remember that. *Bring snacks!*

"Every sound made me more scared," C.J. said. "I opened the tent flap and looked out. It was dark, but I could see shapes in the moonlight."

"Wow."

"Yeah." C.J. pounded his fist into his mitt. "I just watched the lake for a long time. And I remember thinking, 'Devin's parents are right there in the other tent.' I started to feel safer. And it was a beautiful night. I was never *not* scared that night, but it got easier. Sooner or later I fell asleep. Before I knew it, morning arrived."

"It always does, huh?"

C.J. put his arm around Rhino's shoulder. "Every time," he said. "So, enjoy the tournament. Don't complicate things by worrying about being away from home. You'll get through that. Just like I did."

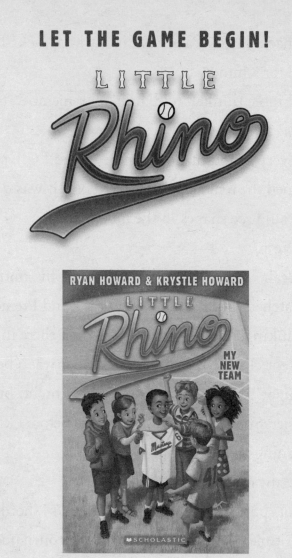

YOU CAN'T HIT WITHOUT A BAT!

BATTER UP WITH
LITTLE RHINO #2!